W9-CCB-477

For my little girl, Zoe

THIS IS A BORZOI BOOK PUBLISHED BY ALFRED A. KNOPF

Visit us on the Web! www.randomhouse.com/kids

Educators and librarians, for a variety of teaching tools, visit us at www.randomhouse.com/teachers

Library of Congress Cataloging-in-Publication Data
Krosoczka, Jarrett.
Ollie / by Jarrett J. Krosoczka. — 1st ed.
p. cm.
Summary: Ollie the purple elephant is delighted to move into the McLaughlin family's New York City apartment, but their cat, Ginger, is not pleased and devises a plan to send Ollie away with the circus.
ISBN 978-0-375-86654-8 (trade) — ISBN 978-0-375-96654-5 (lib. bdg.) — ISBN 978-0-375-98470-9 (ebook)
[1. Elephants—Fiction. 2. Cats—Fiction. 3. Family life—New York (State)—New York—Fiction. 4. Circus—Fiction. 5. New York (N.Y.)—Fiction.] I. Title.
PZ7.K935Oll 2011
[E]—dc22
2010029116

The illustrations in this book were created using acrylic paints on Strathmore illustration board.

MANUFACTURED IN CHINA
October 2011
10 9 8 7 6 5 4 3 2 1

First Edition

the purple elephant

by Jarrett J. Krosoczka

Alfred A. Knopf New York

Mr. McLaughlin had always told his children that should they ever come across a purple elephant, they could keep him. Peter and Shelby so wanted an elephant to call their own.

One day on a stroll through the park, Shelby tugged at her father's shirt and said, "Look, Daddy."

Sure enough, there in the flower garden sat a purple elephant. He was lost and had no place to call home.

Mr. and Mrs. McLaughlin looked at each other in disbelief. “Well . . . a promise is a promise,” said Mr. McLaughlin.

“Mr. Elephant,” said Peter, “would you like to come live with us?”
“That would be nice!” said the elephant. “But please, call me Ollie.”
And that is how Ollie came to live with the McLaughlin family.

Mr. and Mrs. McLaughlin gave Ollie the rules of the house—be nice to one another, no running with scissors, and help with the chores. Ollie was agreeable to these.

The children made up a bed on the fold-out couch in the living room. Ollie didn't have a room to call his own, but he didn't mind. He was happy.

Ollie quickly involved himself in the children's lives.

He enjoyed hopscotch, though he needed some practice.

You would think him a natural at soccer, but he preferred Shelby's ballet lessons.

He also enjoyed kickball, but he was too strong a kicker for his own good. Ollie was especially popular on hot days when the kids needed relief from the heat.

After dinner, the McLaughlin family had impromptu dance parties. Oh, the dance parties they would have! Ollie loved to dance.

But Ginger, the McLaughlins' cat, didn't much care for dancing. She didn't much care for Ollie, for that matter. He had taken her favorite spot on the couch at night.

Mr. Puddlebottom, the McLaughlins' downstairs neighbor, certainly wasn't happy with the new tenant at all.

Over the months, Ginger's disdain for Ollie grew and grew. Finally, she came up with a devious plan.

One evening, Ginger scratched at Mr. Puddlebottom's door. He was particularly cranky, as the dance party upstairs was particularly lively. His foul mood aside, he invited Ginger in for a saucer of milk. She laid out her scheme, and Mr. Puddlebottom's scowl gave way to a wide grin.

"It's brilliant!" he said. "My famous cousin would be delighted to have an extra animal for his show!" And with that, the conspirators shook hands.

That night, when the McLaughlins were all tucked in their beds, Ginger cozied up to Ollie.

"You know, the McLaughlin family regrets ever taking you in."

Naturally, this upset Ollie. The McLaughlins meant the world to him. The thought of being a burden on them broke his heart. "But where could I go?"

"Well," said Ginger, "the circus is in town for one final night. Perhaps they would take you."

Ginger helped Ollie pack his bags.

Ollie left a heartfelt note, apologizing for ever being a problem. But the McLaughlins would never read it, for the second Ollie walked out the front door, Ginger ate the note up!

Peter and Shelby awoke the next day wondering where Ollie was. Perhaps he had gone for a morning jog? When they returned home from school and he was still nowhere to be found, they grew concerned.

By the time they put up "Lost Elephant" posters around the neighborhood, the circus had already left the city.

LOST ELEPHANT

Ringmaster Rankovich ran a tight ship. If his animals weren't performing, they were rehearsing. If they weren't rehearsing, they were traveling.

On these midnight trips, Ollie lay awake chatting with the few friends he had made. Leon the lion, Zoe the monkey, and Ollie shared their dreams, their passions, and stories of the lives they'd left behind.

Life on the road was not easy.

A year later, the circus returned to the city. Opening night came and went with no sign of Peter and Shelby, or Mr. and Mrs. McLaughlin. Night after night, Ollie would look out into the audience for his old family, but they were never there.

After the last performance, Ringmaster Rankovich was feeling generous and gave everyone the night off. Ollie wanted to show Leon and Zoe his old neighborhood. When they arrived at Ollie's apartment building . . .

. . . it was being **robbed!**

Ollie needed to do something—and **fast!**

Ollie kicked over a fire hydrant, sucked up all the water his trunk could hold, and blasted the crooks! Leon roared to scare the robbers, waking the sleeping tenants, while Zoe nabbed the stolen goods!

The police were soon on the scene and arrested the robbers. All of the curious tenants took to the streets—including the McLaughlin family.

"OLLIE!" yelled Peter and Shelby. "Oh, how we've missed you! Why did you leave us? Please come home again!"

Their affection took Ollie by surprise. "I'd love to," he said. "You'd have me back?"

“There will be none of that!” snarled Ringmaster Rankovich as he stepped onto the scene. “Come now, my circus animals. To the circus cart. It’s off to the next town!”

“But I’d like to stay here with my family,” said Ollie.

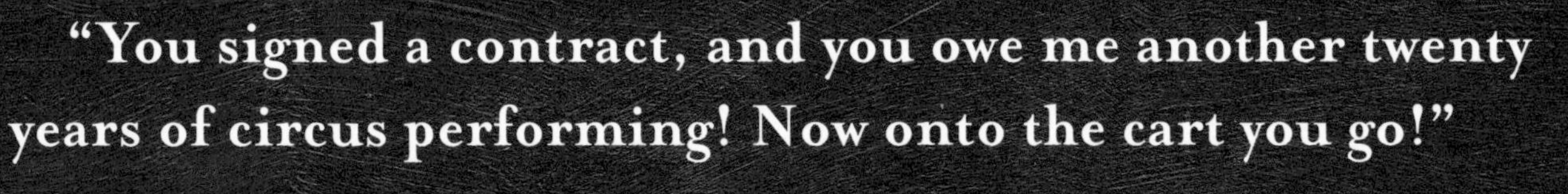

"You signed a contract, and you owe me another twenty years of circus performing! Now onto the cart you go!"

"But I don't remember signing any contracts," thought a puzzled Ollie.

Mr. McLaughlin snatched the contract away. Upon quick inspection, he proclaimed, "*This* is a forgery and I can prove it! I happen to be the landlord of this building, and every month I receive a check signed by one Mr. Puddlebottom. The handwriting on your contract is Mr. Puddlebottom's, *not* Ollie's!"

Everyone was shocked. But not as shocked as Mr. Puddlebottom and Ringmaster Rankovich! The cousins had been caught red-handed!

"So, Ollie," Mr. McLaughlin asked, "won't you please come back and live with us?"

"Absolutely!" cheered Ollie. Then he thought of something. "What about my friends from the circus? Could they live here, too?"

The police drove away with Ringmaster Rankovich and Mr. Puddlebottom. “Well, it does look like we’ll have an open apartment,” said Mrs. McLaughlin.

And so—much to the chagrin of Ginger—Ollie the elephant, Leon the lion, and Zoe the monkey all moved in. They lived in the apartment just below the McLaughlin family, with whom they had many dance parties.

Both upstairs and down.